S0-EBU-387

KALEIDOSCOPE

The Sun

Dan Elish

Marshall Cavendish
Benchmark
New York

Marshall Cavendish Benchmark
99 White Plains Road
Tarrytown, New York 10591-9001
www.marshallcavendish.us

Library of Congress Cataloging-in-Publication Data
Elish, Dan.
The sun / by Dan Elish.
p. cm. — (Kaleidoscope)
Includes bibliographical references and index.
ISBN-13: 978-0-7614-2048-4
ISBN-10: 0-7614-2048-7
1. Sun—Juvenile literature. I. Title. II. Series: Kaleidoscope (Tarrytown, N.Y.)
QB521.5.E45 2006 523.7—dc22 2006003228

Editor: Marilyn Mark
Editorial Director: Michelle Bisson
Art Director: Anahid Hamparian
Series Designer: Adam Mietlowski

Photo Research by Anne Burns Images
Cover Photo by Photri-Microstock

The photographs in this book are used with permission and through the courtesy of: *Photo Researchers, Inc.*: pp. 1, 28 Detlev Van Ravenswaay/Science Photo Library; p. 16 Russell Kightley; p. 24 Scharmer et al/Royal Swedish Academy/Science Photo Library; p. 31 John Chumack/Science Photo Library; p. 35 Lynette Cook. *Art Resource*: p. 4 Werner Forman; p. 5 Erich Lessing. *Bridgeman Art Library*: p. 8 The Stapleton Collection. *Julian Baum*: p. 11. *Corbis*: pp. 12, 15 Royalty Free; p. 27 Bettman; p. 36 Rolf Bruderer. *Photri-Microstock*: pp. 19, 23, 32, 39, 40, 43. *NASA/JPL*: p. 20

Printed in Malaysia
6 5 4 3 2 1

Contents

The Myth of the Sun

Since the beginning of time, people have been fascinated by the Sun. The people of ancient Egypt believed that the Sun God, Ra, created the world and was the master of all life.

◀ *This wall painting, found in the tomb of Nefertari in Thebes, Egypt, shows a union between the Sun God, Ra, and Osiris, the god of death and resurrection. Osiris is depicted as the ram-headed mummy with the sun disk, representing Ra, between the horns.*

Ancient Greeks believed that a god named Helios rode a golden chariot across the sky each morning to bring sunlight to the world.

Helios is shown on his golden horse-drawn chariot. This Greek artwork was found on a vase in Canosa di Pulia, Italy, and is from 330 BCE.

In the United States, Native Americans paid respect to the Sun through energetic Sun Dances that sometimes lasted as long as eight days.

These cultures clearly understood that our planet depends on the Sun for just about everything. The Sun is Earth's star, and its heat supplies the energy that allows all life on Earth to grow and thrive.

◀ *This nineteenth-century artwork depicts the Shoshone Sun Dance. The pole in the center symbolizes the Sun. The Shoshone Indians lived both east and west of the Rocky Mountains. Other North American Indian nations, such as the Cheyenne and Sioux, also held ceremonies that included a Sun Dance.*

A Swirl of Space Dust

Scientists believe that about 5 billion years ago a dark cloud of dust and vapor floated into our galaxy. It began to form into a giant rotating cloud of gas. As the cloud whirled faster and faster, the dust and gas collided and the inner *core* grew extremely hot. Ten million years later the core reached a temperature of 27 million degrees Fahrenheit (15 million degrees Celsius)! At this great heat, a series of *nuclear reactions* were set off. Nuclear reactions occur when particles smaller than an atom, called *protons*, collide and release giant amounts of energy.

Our Sun was created, along with the nine planets. The remaining space dust came together in the same way to form our Solar System.

This artist's rendering shows the birth of the Sun, created by a chain of nuclear reactions that scientists believe created the Sun and our Solar System. ▶

A Yellow Dwarf

Around 75 percent of the Sun is made up of the most common element in the universe. It is a colorless, highly *flammable* (easily set on fire) gas called *hydrogen*. In 1868 *astronomer* Jules Janssen discovered that most of the rest of the Sun is made up of *helium*, an element commonly found in the *atmosphere* of stars. Atmosphere is the mass of air or gases that surround a planet or a star.

◀ *Helium, a common element found in the Sun and in the atmosphere of stars, is used to make balloons float.*

If you were lying on a beach on a summer day, the Sun might seem fairly close, but those rays would actually be coming from 93 million miles (about 150 million kilometers) away! Though the Sun may look no bigger than a silver dollar floating in the sky, it is almost too big to believe. It would take 109 Earths lined up side by side to stretch across the Sun's face. Or imagine: the Earth could fit inside the Sun's interior almost a million and a half times. It is equally amazing to realize that the Sun is only one star, like billions of others in our Solar System, the Milky Way. Some stars, such as the Sun, are big while others are small. Astronomers call the most common stars *yellow dwarves.*

Our Sun may seem to be very close to this family on the beach, but it is actually 93 million miles (150 million km) away. ▶

The Many-Layered Star

Through years of study, astronomers have been able to learn a lot about how the Sun creates its great heat. It all starts in the Sun's center, or its core, which is surrounded by two walls of gas, called the *radiative zone* and the *convective zone*. Temperatures at the core reach 29 million degrees F (16 million degrees C). Due to this heat and high pressure, 700 million tons (635 billion kilograms) of hydrogen are converted into 695 million tons (630 billion kg) of helium every second. As a result of this process, called *nuclear fusion*, 5 million tons (4.5 billion kg) of energy are released into the Solar System every second.

◀ *This cutaway diagram shows the layers of the Sun. The Sun's core is blue, the radioactive zone is yellow-green, and the convective zone is orange.*

All that heat travels up through the Sun to its *photosphere*, which is the visible surface of the Sun. The temperature on this outer layer is 11,000 degrees F (6,094 degrees C). Each square centimeter emits as much light as a 6,000-watt lamp. Right above the photosphere is the *chromosphere*, an area of the Sun that is almost completely *transparent*, or see-through. This is where solar energy flows into the Solar System from the center of the Sun.

This artwork depicts the photosphere, the visible surface of the Sun, and the chromosphere, the invisible surface of the Sun from which solar energy flows into our Solar System. The Sun's strong magnetic forces are shown. They can affect Earth and the entire Solar System. ▶

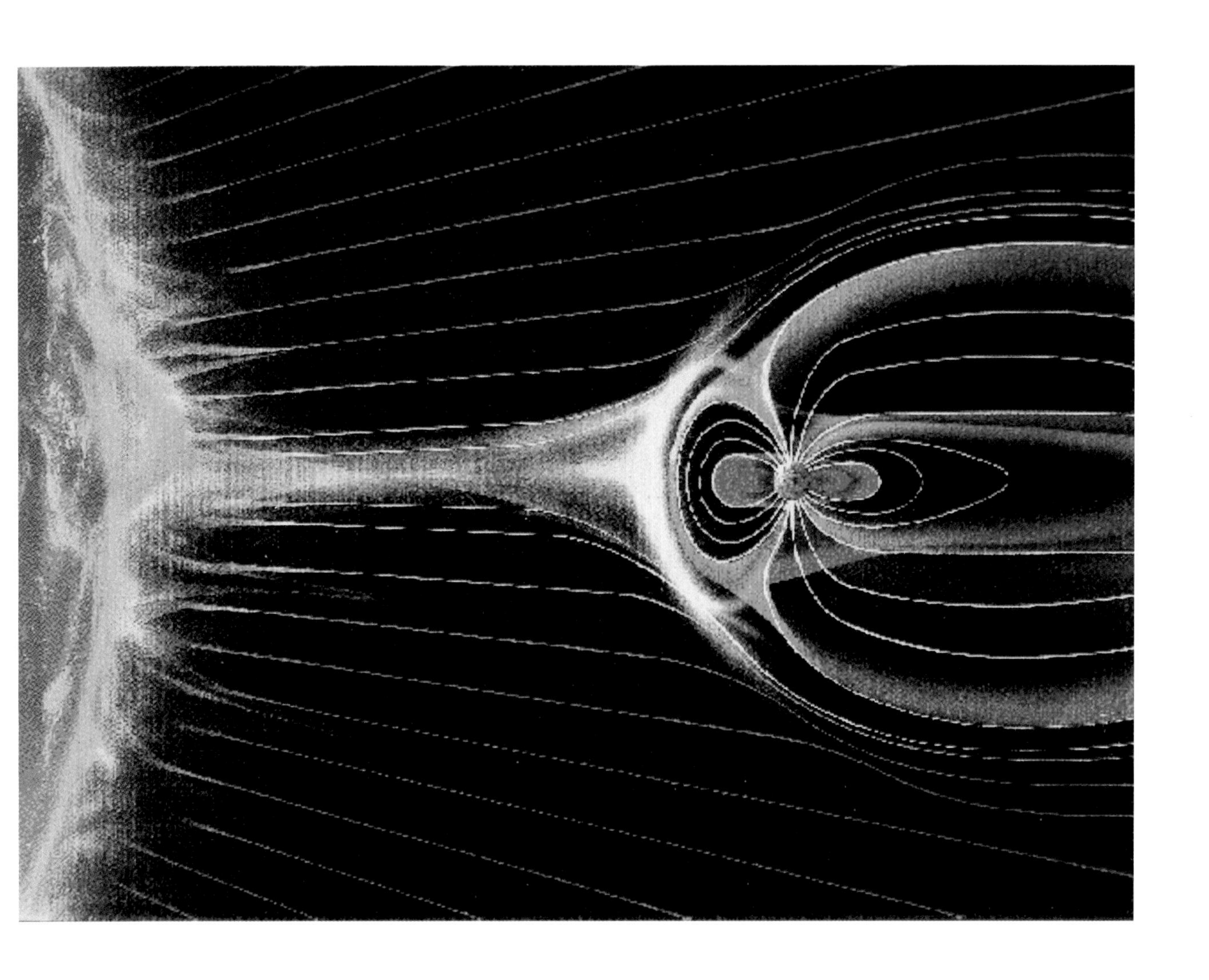

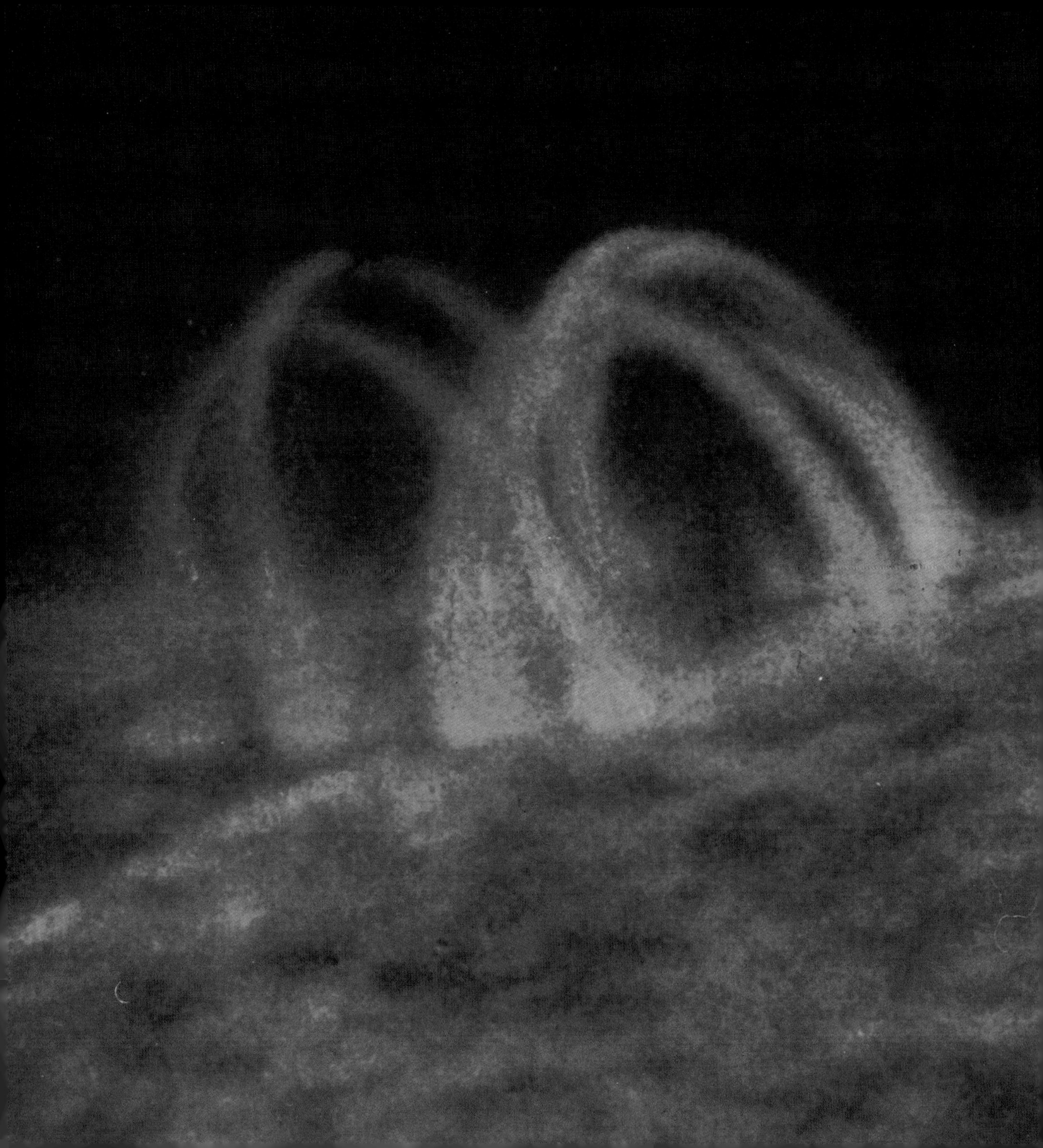

The Sun's atmosphere is called the *corona*. The corona is visible from Earth only during a total solar eclipse when the Moon blocks the Sun's light. But the corona is something to see! Giant walls of flame called *spicules* fly out of the photosphere and feed hot gas to the corona. In fact, the temperature of the corona is five hundred times hotter than on the Sun's surface, or a whopping one million degrees F (555,582 degrees C).

◀ *Here we can see a close-up of the spicules, or walls of flame, flying out of the photosphere. These magnetic loops feed hot gas to the corona.*

Since heat usually rises, astronomers still are not sure how it is possible that the corona is so much hotter than the Sun's surface. Some think this phenomenon has to do with a series of unusual *magnetic fields* on the Sun's surface.

This model shows the unusual magnetic fields on the surface of the Sun. The corona is the green and white plane in the foreground of the image, which was taken by the Extreme Ultraviolet Imaging Telescope (EIT). There are about fifty thousand of these high-energy magnetic fields on the surface of the Sun at any one time, and they shift, appear, and disappear about every forty hours. ▶

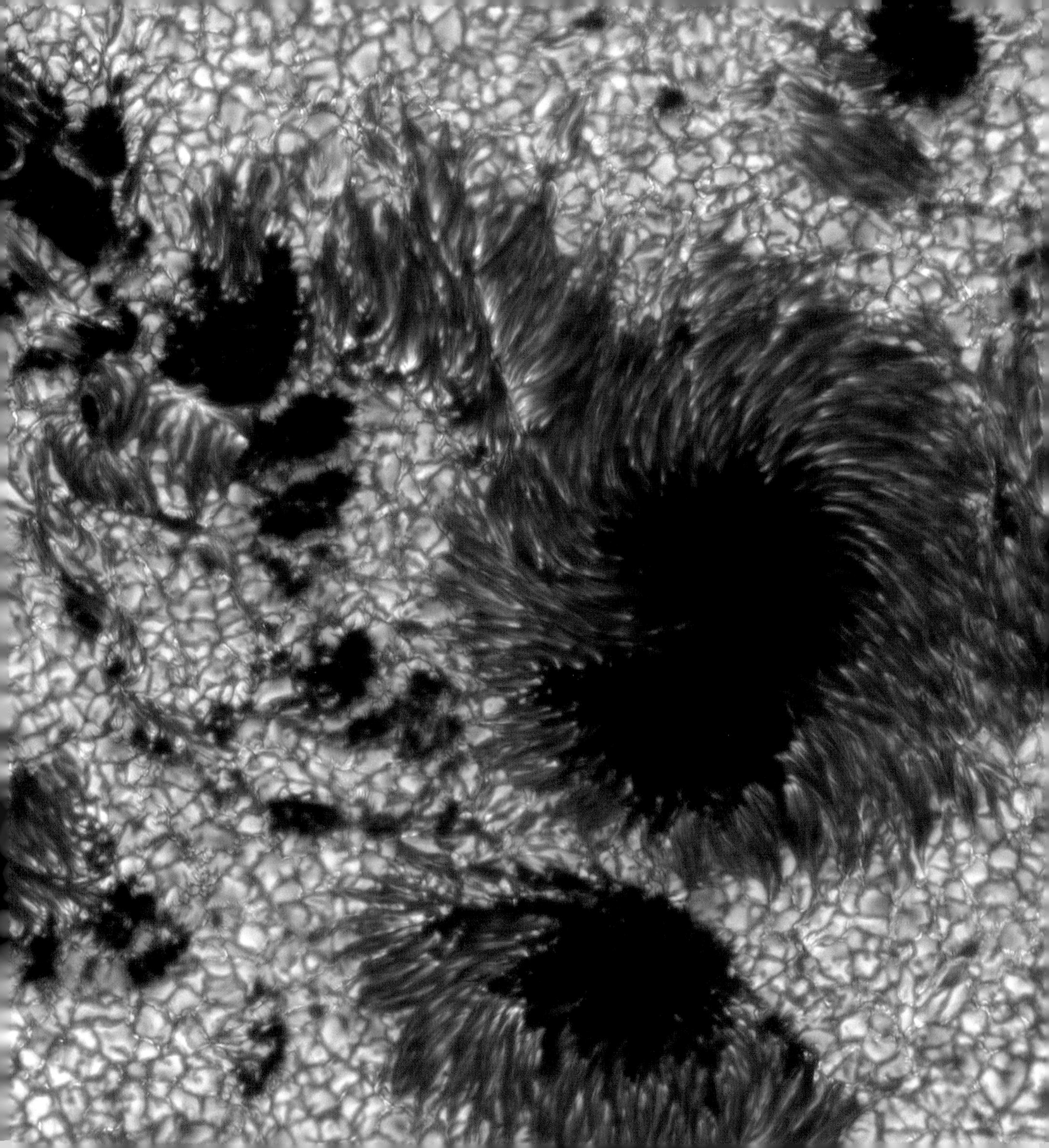

Some astronomers also believe that the Sun's complex magnetic fields help create *sunspots*. These are small, dark blotches that appear on the face of the photosphere. First reported by Chinese astronomers as long ago as 200 BCE, these spots are usually cooler than the rest of the Sun. They can be as wide as 30,000 miles (48,280 km) in diameter. The largest sunspot ever reported was in April 1947. It was thirty-five times the surface area of Earth! Through the study of sunspots, scientists have figured out that different parts of the Sun rotate at different speeds.

◀ *These sunspots, cooler regions on the Sun's surface, are shown up close. Scientists believe that sunspots are formed by powerful magnetic fields that cross the photosphere. The number of sunspots on the Sun changes about every eleven years, but scientists are not sure why.*

Though astronomers do not know what causes sunspots to appear, evidence suggests that they might have a direct effect on the Earth's weather. From 1450 to 1850, the average temperatures in Europe were so low that people living at that time referred to it as the Little Ice Age. In 1690 children could ice skate on London's Thames River, and Amsterdam's canals froze. In 1976, an astronomer named Jack Eddy realized that the Little Ice Age took place at a time when there were no sunspots. As a result, most astronomers now believe that the absence of sunspots cools the Earth.

During the Little Ice Age, there were no sunspots on the Sun and temperatures in Europe were so low that the Thames River and Amsterdam's canals froze. This woodcut depicts a "frost fair" on the Thames River in London during the winter of 1683–1684. Booths were set up on the frozen river between Southwark and Temple. ▶

Arundel-House.
Essex-Buildings.
The Temple.

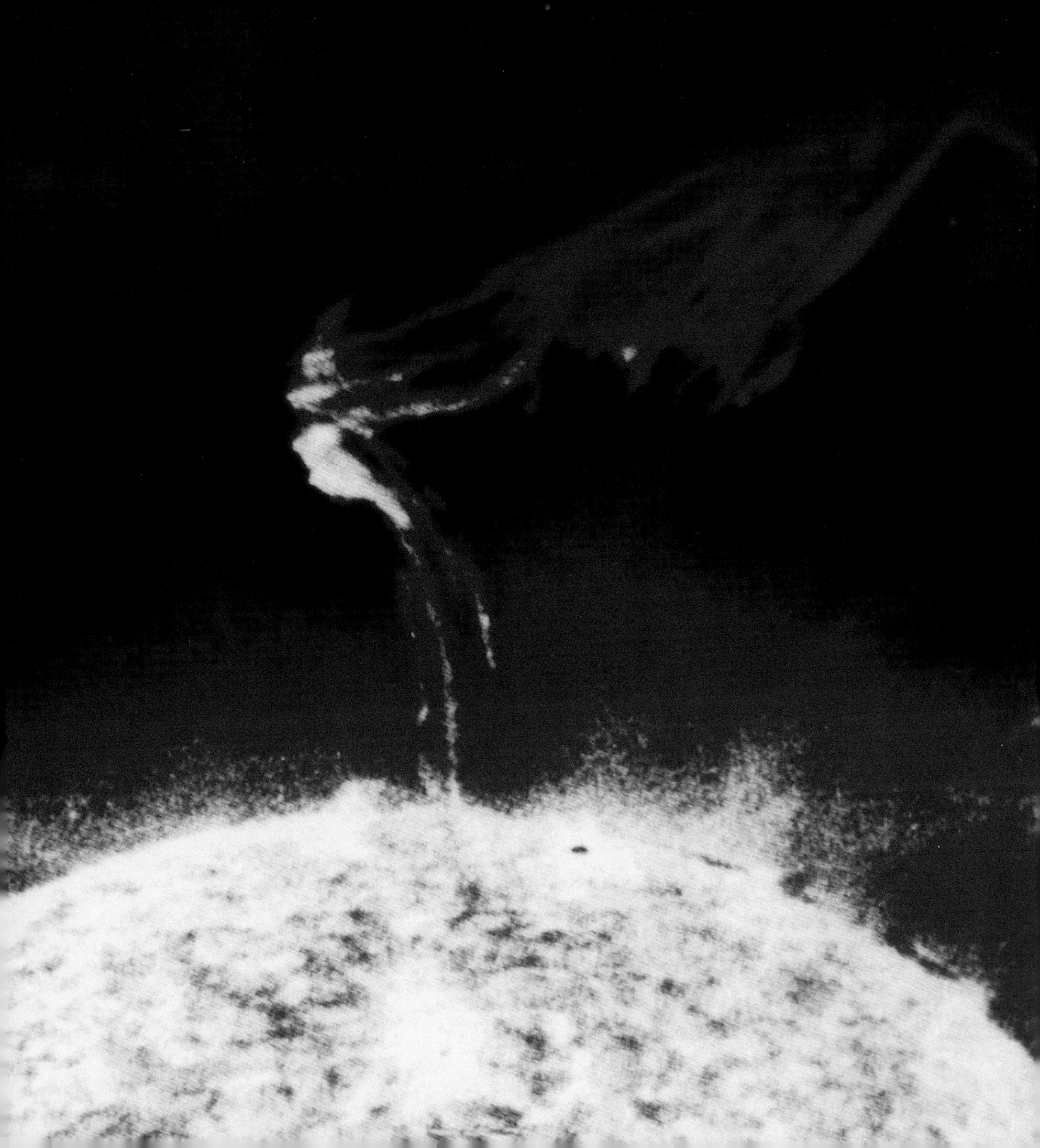

The Sun affects life on Earth in countless ways. In addition to heat and light, the Sun also sends a constant stream of charged particles into the galaxy. This is called the *solar wind*. Traveling through the Solar System at 281 miles (452 km) per second, the solar wind can interfere with radio waves when it reaches Earth's atmosphere.

◀ *This image, taken by the space station* Skylab, *shows a solar flare, which becomes a part of the solar wind when it erupts. The solar wind is a stream of charged particles that the Sun sends into the galaxy.*

The solar wind is also the cause of the *northern lights*, or "aurora borealis," one of the most beautiful natural wonders on the planet. When the solar wind hits Earth's North and South Poles at high speeds, the sky becomes streaked with gorgeous color.

Northern lights, also called aurora borealis, are seen here in Fairborn-Enon, Ohio. This beautiful phenomenon is caused by the Sun's solar wind. ▶

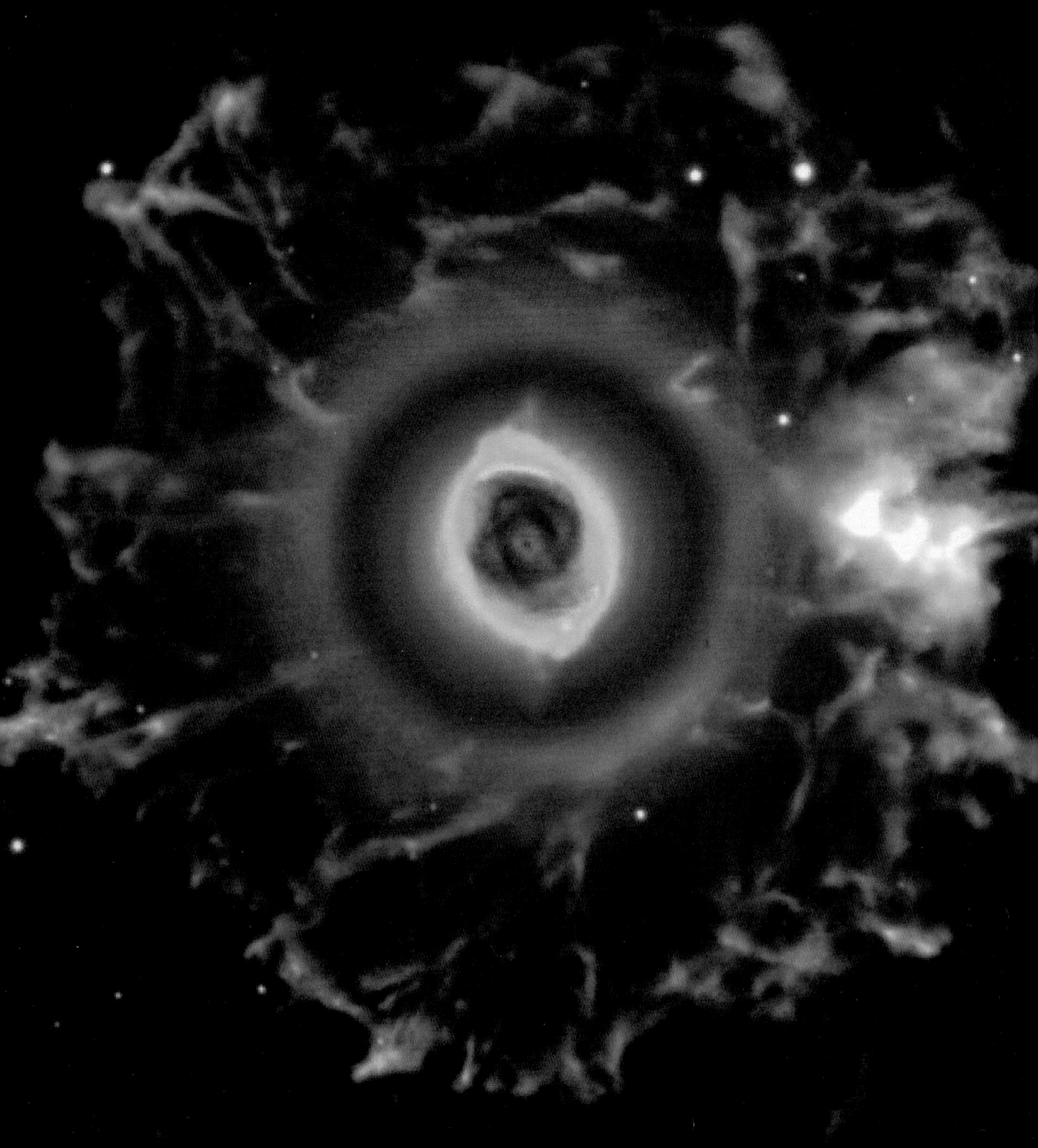

Life Span of the Sun

Even though the Sun is already about 4.5 billion years old, it still has a lot of life left in it. Astronomers believe that the Sun has enough gas left to continue lighting up the sky for another 5 billion years. But when its hydrogen and helium have been used up, the Sun will begin to swell. It will then turn into an enormous star called a *red giant*. At this point, the Sun's outer layers will continue to expand and drift off into space, forming what astronomers call a *planetary nebula*.

◀ *As a star's layers expand and drift into space, it becomes a planetary nebula, such as the one seen here—the Cat's Eye Nebula—which is one of the most famous.*

As most of its mass is dispersed into the Solar System, the Sun's core will shrink. Eventually, the Sun will become a *white dwarf*, or a smaller, more stable star. By then it will only be 1,000 miles (1,609 km) in diameter. The Sun will give off the last of its heat for billions of years. When it has finally cooled, it will become a *black dwarf*, which is a cold, dead star.

A white dwarf, or dying star, is shown in the upper-middle part of this artwork. ▶

Spaceships to the Sun

When astronomers want to learn more about the Sun, they cannot go there—not unless they have spacesuits that can withstand temperatures of more than one million degrees F (555,582 degrees C)! It is also very dangerous to look directly at the Sun for more than a quick second. The bright rays can cause severe eye damage or even blindness.

◀ *Sunglasses are important protection for your eyes against the Sun's bright rays on a sunny day. Even with sunglasses, though, it is dangerous to look directly at the Sun.*

Luckily, over the past decade, the world's scientists have had great success creating a series of spacecraft specially designed to investigate the Sun. In October 1990 the spacecraft *Ulysses* was launched from the space shuttle *Discovery*. It is the only spacecraft to have visited the *heliosphere*, the magnetic bubble containing our Solar System, the solar wind, and the entire solar magnetic field. Due to *Ulysses*' unique orbit, astronomers have discovered that the Sun's solar wind blows much faster near its polar regions. *Ulysses*, which collected data about the Sun for twelve years, also measured the Sun's energy output and found that it has stayed constant for many years.

The Ulysses *spacecraft, shown here, is the only spacecraft to have explored the region over the Sun's poles.* ▶

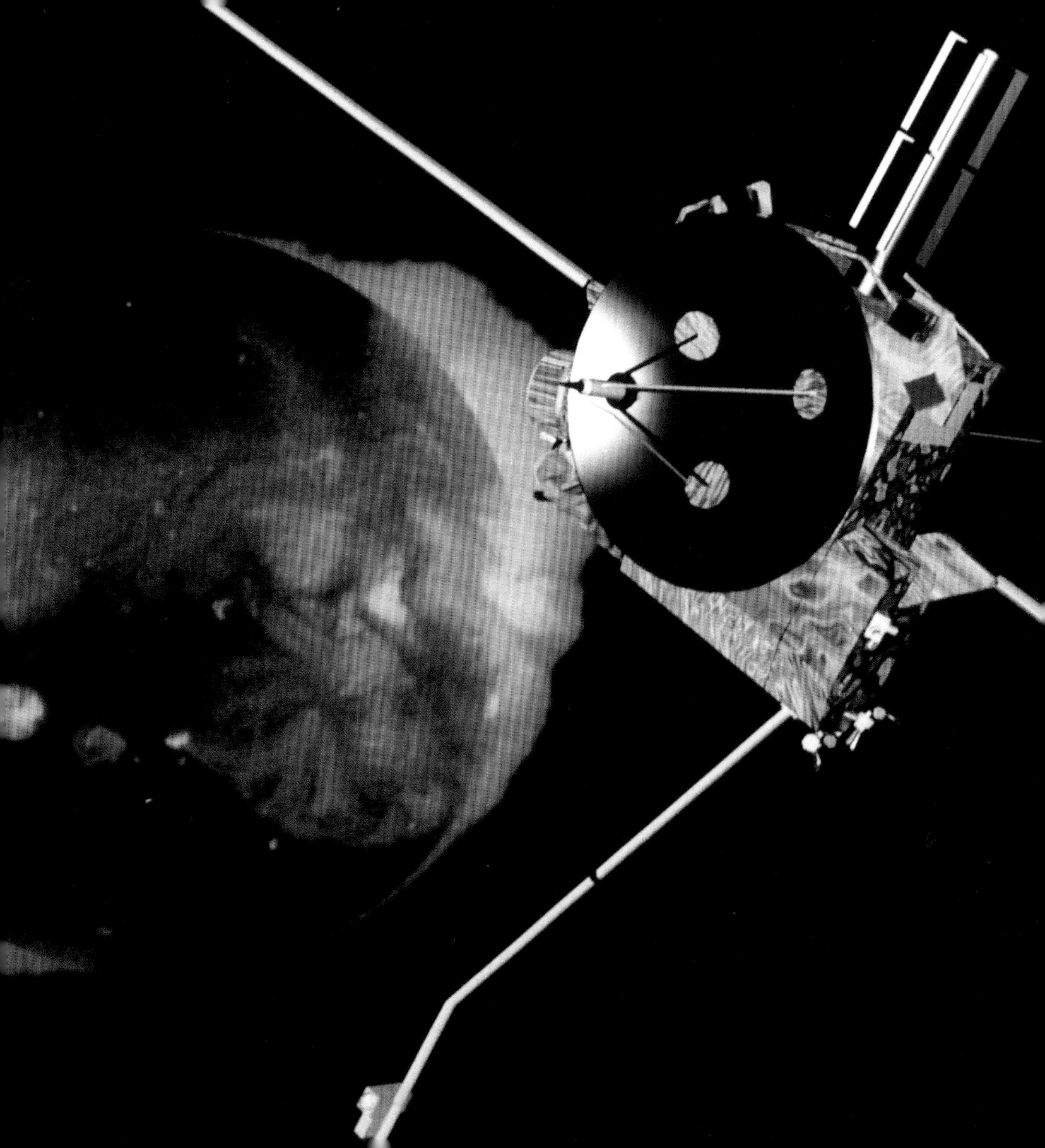

esa

In 1995 American and European space agencies launched *SOHO* (Solar and Heliospheric Observatory), a spacecraft *observatory*. This craft contains twelve specialized instruments designed to study the internal structure of the Sun and its complex outer atmosphere. Best of all, the Sun itself never sets on *SOHO*. Coasting one million miles (1,609,000 km) from Earth (or four times the distance to the Moon), *SOHO* allows astronomers to study the Sun twenty-four hours a day.

◀ *This photograph shows* SOHO, *a spacecraft observatory that uses twelve different instruments to study the Sun.*

Solar Energy: The Future

One of the major tasks facing the world today is protecting Earth's environment. Each year, thousands of tons of oil and gasoline are burned for energy, polluting the planet. But there may be a solar solution. Scientists have been looking at ways to harness the Sun's energy to produce the electricity needed to power everything from industrial machinery to cars. Today, *photovoltaic electricity* is produced by a machine that turns solar radiation into electricity, bringing us closer to a future that relies more on the Sun's energy than on Earth's fossil fuels, such as oil and gas.

Though scientists are still working on solutions, there is reason to hope that in the future most of Earth's energy needs will be met by using our own unique power source—the Sun.

These machines collect direct solar radiation, which can then be turned into photovoltaic electricity. ▶

Glossary

astronomers—Scientists who study the universe.
atmosphere—The layer of gas that surrounds a star or planet.
black dwarf—A cold, dead star.
chromosphere—The transparent layer just outside the Sun's surface.
convective zone—Along with the radiative zone, one of the thick shells of gas at the Sun's core.
core—The center of the Sun.
corona—The Sun's atmosphere.
flammable—Something that can be set on fire easily.
heliosphere—The immense magnetic bubble containing our Solar System, the solar wind, and the entire solar magnetic field.
helium—A gas commonly found in the atmospheres of stars that makes up about 25 percent of the Sun.
hydrogen—A colorless, flammable gas that is the most common element in the universe. Hydrogen makes up about 75 percent of the Sun.
magnetic fields—The state in which there are magnetic forces at every point of a certain region.
northern lights—The wash of color that lights up the night sky in the northern and southern regions of the planet when the solar wind hits Earth's atmosphere. Also called *aurora borealis*.
nuclear fusion—The process in which hydrogen is converted into helium due to high heat and high pressure.
nuclear reaction—The process in which subatomic particles collide, giving off massive amounts of energy.

observatory—A scientific laboratory devoted to studying the universe.
photosphere—The Sun's yellow surface.
photovoltaic electricity—A type of electricity that is produced by collecting the Sun's energy.
planetary nebula—The state of a star after its outer layers expand and drift off into space.
protons—Subatomic particles.
radiative zone—Along with the convective zone, one of the thick shells of gas at the Sun's core.
red giant—An enormous star that has used up its hydrogen and helium.
solar wind—A stream of charged particles that the Sun sends into the Solar System.
spicules—Pillars of flame that fly out of the Sun's photosphere and feed hot gas into the corona.
sunspots—Dark blotches that occasionally appear on the Sun and are much cooler than the rest of the Sun.
transparent—See-through.
white dwarf—A stable star with no nuclear fuel.
yellow dwarf—The most common kind of star in the universe.

Find Out More

Books

Carlowicz, Michael J., and Ramon E. Lopez. *Storms from the Sun: The Emerging Science of Space Weather*. Washington, DC: Joseph Henry Press, 2002.

Ford, Harry. *The Young Astronomer*. New York: Dorling Kindersley, 1998.

Gifford, Clive. *Facts and Records Book of Space*. New York: Kingfisher, 2001.

Mitton, Jacqueline, and Simon Mitton. *The Scholastic Encyclopedia of Space*. New York: Scholastic, 1998.

Wilson, Christina. *The Solar System, An A–Z Guide*. New York: Franklin Watts, 2000.

Zirker, Jack B. *Journey from the Center of the Sun*. Princeton, NJ: Princeton University Press, 2002.

Web Sites

General Information on the Sun
http://seds.lpl.arizona.edu/nineplanets/nineplanets/sol.html
http://starchild.gsfc.nasa.gov/docs/StarChild/solar_system_level1/sun.html

Information on *Ulysses*
http://ulysses.jpl.nasa.gov/

Layers of the Sun
http://fusedweb.pppl.gov/CPEP/Chart_Pages/5.Plasmas/SunLayers.html

SOHO—Solar and Heliospheric Observatory
http://sohowww.nascom.nasa.gov

The Sun—A Multimedia Tour
http://www.michielb.nl/sun/kaft.htm

About the Author

Dan Elish has written a variety of fiction and nonfiction books for children, including *The Trail of Tears: The Story of the Cherokee Removal*, in Marshall Cavendish's Great Journeys series, which was hailed as an "excellent resource" by *School Library Journal*. He also wrote *Born Too Short, The Confessions of an 8th Grade Basket Case*, which was picked as a Book for the Teen Age in 2003 by the New York Public Library and also won an International Reading Association Students' Choice Award. In addition to that, Dan is an accomplished scriptwriter for television. He lives in New York City with his wife and daughter.

Index

Page numbers for illustrations are in **boldface.**